LUCÍA the LUCHADORA

By
Cynthia Leonor Garza

Illustrated by
Alyssa Bermudez

SCHOLASTIC INC.

I zip through the playground in my red cape.

POW

I go POW.

I go BAM.

BAM

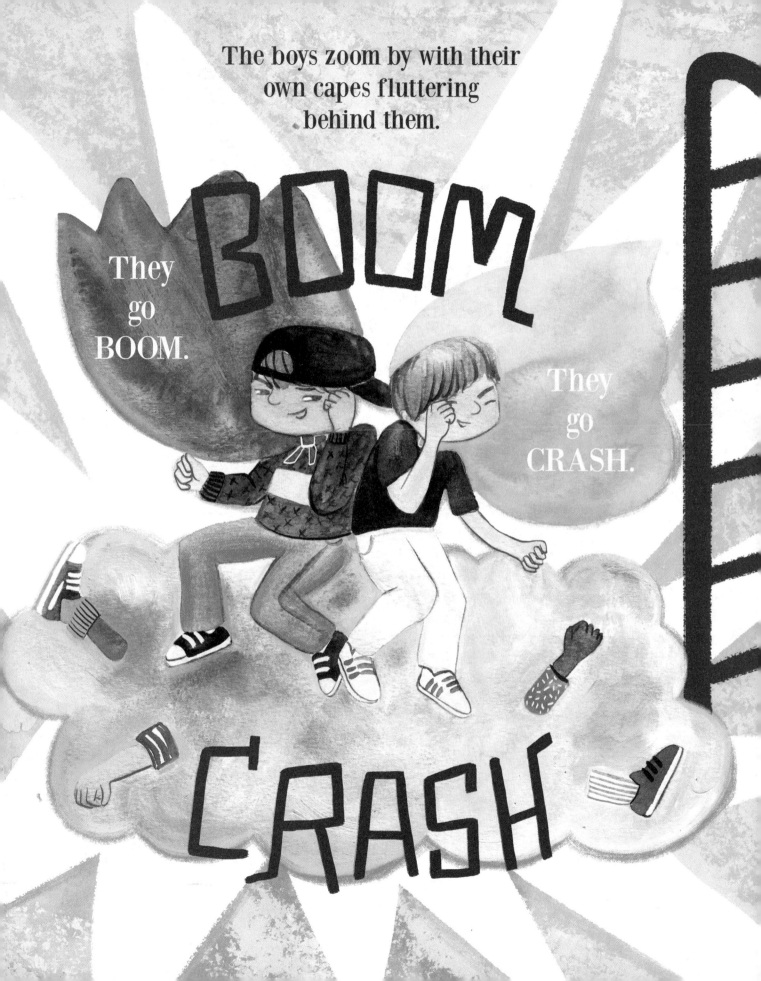

The boys try to jump off the monkey bars,
but no one can do a high-flying leap from the top like I can.
I dive. I spin. I nail my landing.
Every! Single! Time!

I dash up
the dark,
swirly slide
that no one
dares go near,
but the
boys pay
no attention
to me.

I don't feel very nice and sweet at that moment.
I feel mad. Spicy mad. KA-POW kind of mad!

Abuela watches me from a nearby bench.
When I flop down next to her, Abu leans over
and whispers a secret. We hatch a plan.

That night, Abu gives me an old box.
There's a shiny, satin cape inside,
and a very special silver mask.

Abu tells me that when she was a little girl,
she was a special kind of superhero,
a luchadora.

I don't know what a luchadora is.
Abu tells me a luchadora is more than a
masked wrestler with swift moves, more
than just a superhero with slick style.
A luchadora is agile.
She moves and thinks quickly.

A luchadora has moxie. She is brave and full of heart, and isn't afraid to fight for what is right. Most importantly, a luchadora never reveals her **true identity**.

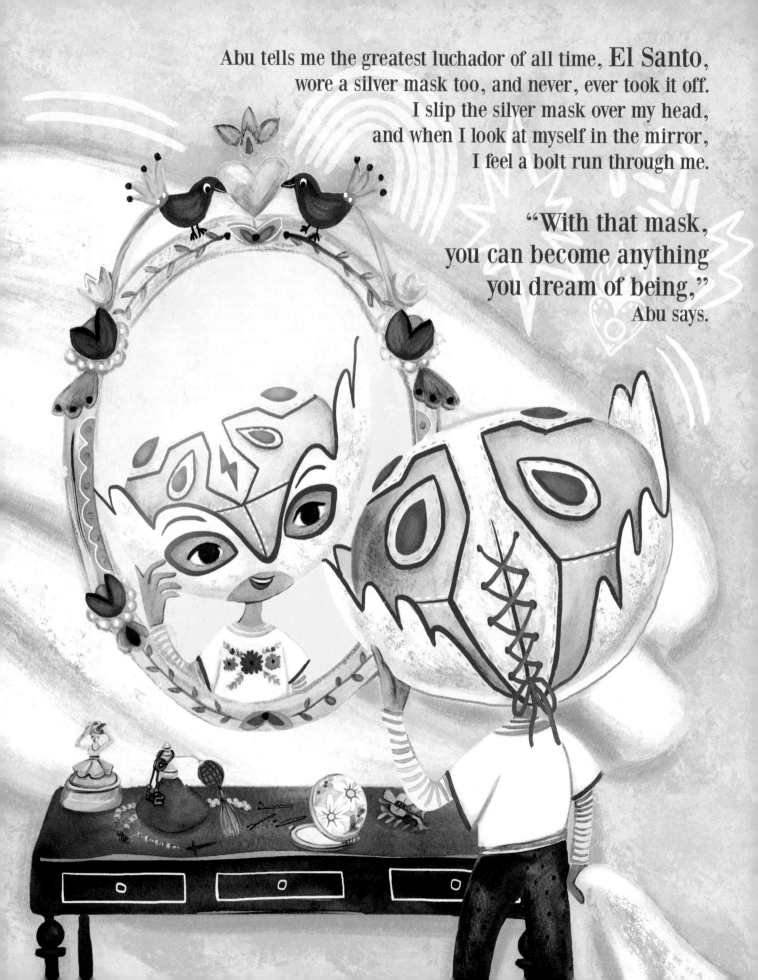

Abu tells me the greatest luchador of all time, El Santo,
wore a silver mask too, and never, ever took it off.
I slip the silver mask over my head,
and when I look at myself in the mirror,
I feel a bolt run through me.

"With that mask,
you can become anything
you dream of being,"
Abu says.

WHOMP

WHAM

On the playground the next day, the boys zoom by in their capes.

They go WHAM.

They go WHOMP.

I charge through the crowd, my new silver and white cape a blinding flash behind me.

I catch everyone's eyes. Everyone wants to know who is wearing the silver mask. I'm a luchadora with a secret identity.

With my silver mask, I can become anything I dream of being.

I stand on the top of the monkey bars,

ready to do my high-flying leap.

I dive. I spin.

I nail my landing, like always.

This time, everyone notices.

BOOM

CRASH

The crowd goes wild!
The boys go BOOM.
They try to
CRASH into me.

But I'm lightning fast,
and no one can catch me.
No one can wow like I can.

I am the best kind of superhero.
I'm Lucía the Luchadora!

Before long,
I see lots of other
lucha libre masks
on the playground.

One day, I spot a crusader in
a pink mask with red glittery hearts.
A girl! Another luchadora!
I can't wait to play
with the new pink crusader.

But before I can run over,
I hear something familiar.

Just then,
the dark,
swirly slide
goes CLANG.
Everyone stops
and stares.
BANG.
JANGLE.
SCRITCH!

Everyone shrinks, but I move closer.

I hear a YIP and a YELP and a peep that sounds like HELP! I feel the TICK-TOCK in my chest, but I don't flinch. I dash through the crowd and up the ladder.

WHEE!

Moments later, I swoop down the slide
with Little Coco in my lap.
BRAVO, everyone cheers.
My heart swells! But then,
I spot the pink crusader in the crowd.
Why does she look so sad?

I remember Abu's words:
**A real luchadora must fight
for what is right.**

My heart doesn't feel very
full anymore.
I know what I have to do.
I pull off my mask.

ZAP!
Everyone is
thunderstruck.
My true identity
is revealed.
I am no longer
a luchadora.

Then, something
unexpected happens.
**CLAP, CLAP,
CLAP**

Then, something SPECTACULAR happens.
Luchadoras everywhere, hidden in plain sight!

Little Coco jumps off my lap
and races through the crowd.

I bolt after him in a flash,
and all the boys and girls
start to chase me.

But I'm lightning fast, and no one can catch me.
No one is as dazzling or daring as I am.

I climb up the monkey bars. I dive. I spin.
And when I strike the ground, a charge runs through the crowd.

I am still
the best kind
of superhero.

I am
Lucía
the Luchadora,
mask or no mask.

A note on
luchadoras, luchadores,
and
lucha libre

Luchadores* are the larger-than-life stars
of the world of lucha libre – the acrobatic and
theatrical style of wrestling popularized in Mexico.
Many wear masks to help conceal their true identities,
although they can be unmasked by their opponent if they
lose a match. Luchadores fall into two camps, the heroes and
villains, or *técnicos* and *rudos*, and fight as individuals or in
teams in the ring. Often, lucha matches follow lively storylines
filled with twists and turns. But the stories of good versus evil
don't end in the ring. The adventures of some of the most popular
luchadores have leapt beyond the ring and into comic books,
films, and even the streets, where luchadores have transformed
themselves into real-life masked heroes fighting for social
justice. Luchadores have fought and advocated for many causes,
including animals, the environment, and the rights of poor
people, children, women, and those living in substandard
housing. On the flip side, women have long fought – and
are still fighting – for their place in the wrestling ring in
the largely male-dominated sport. Over the past few
decades, many fierce luchadoras have paved a
dazzling path into the world of lucha libre
and have claimed their spots among
the stars.

*In Spanish, the word "luchadores" is used when talking about only male, or both male
and female lucha libre wrestlers. The word "luchadoras" refers only to female wrestlers.

For Kalila and Estela
— C.L.G.

Lucía the Luchadora

No part of this publication may be reproduced, stored in a retrieval system, or transmitted in any form or by any means, electronic, mechanical, photocopying, recording, or otherwise, without written permission of the publisher. For information regarding permission, write to POW!, 32 Adams Street, Brooklyn, NY 11201.

ISBN 978-1-338-31453-3

12 11 10 9 8 7 6 5 4 3 2 1   18 19 20 21 22 23

Printed in the U.S.A.   40

First Scholastic printing, October 2018

Book design: Krzysztof Poluchowicz